# The Coolest Place in Town

**Kathy Caple**

Houghton Mifflin Company

Boston 1990

To my parents,
Verle and Jean Caple

Library of Congress Cataloging-in-Publication Data

Caple, Kathy.
The coolest place in town / Kathy Caple.
   p.   cm.
   Summary: When Hank and Zoey's sister Dory kicks them out of their wading pool on a hot summer day, the two boys find a way to get even.
   ISBN 0-395-51523-8
   [1. Swimming pools – Fiction. 2. Brothers and sisters – Fiction.]
I. Title.
PZ7.C17368Han   1990        89-24447
[E]–dc20                     CIP
                            AC

It was the hottest day of the whole summer.
Hank and Zoey had done nothing but complain.
"It's already over 100 degrees," said Hank.
"I'm melting," said his brother, Zoey.

"Let's cool off in the cellar," said Hank.

"What a creepy place," said Zoey.

"What's that round blue tub?" asked Hank.

"Oh that's the pool we used
when we were  babies," said Zoey.
"Let's try it," said Hank.

They carried the pool out to the backyard

and filled it with water.

· It was the coolest place in town.

Just then their sister, Dory, came out.

"Na, na, look at the babies.  Boy do you look dumb.

I haven't been in one of those since I was two

years old.  I'm going to the town pool.  Too bad.

Babies aren't allowed."

"Just ignore her," said Hank.

He went into the house to get some things.

Hank came back with two snorkels and face masks.
He tossed some shells into the pool.

Hank and Zoey looked at the shells.

"Everything looks bigger under water," said Zoey.
Just then they heard a noise. They looked up.

"I'm back," said Dory.  "The town pool was too crowded."
She was drinking some fruit punch.

"Can we have some?" asked Hank.
"There's more in the refrigerator," said Dory.

Hank and Zoey ran into the house.

"I don't see any punch," said Hank.

"We've been tricked," said Zoey.

They hurried back outside.

Dory was sitting in the pool.

"Get out of our pool," said Hank.

"You said it was for babies."

"I changed my mind," said Dory.

Hank and Zoey tried tipping her out of the pool.
But she was too heavy.

Then they grabbed her foot and pulled.
It was no use.

"Give us back our pool," said Zoey.
"You can have it all winter," said Dory.

Hank and Zoey went to the front porch and sat down.
"We have to think of something," said Hank.

"We could scare her out with this shark," said Zoey.
"She's not afraid of sharks," said Hank.
"Let's bomb her out," said Zoey.

They ran inside and got some balloons.

They filled the balloons with water.

They hid behind the bushes

and aimed very carefully.

SPLAT! Hank hit Dory with the first balloon.

"Feels good, *Hankerchief*," she said.

Zoey threw another.

Dory ducked. The balloon went through a window.

"Who threw that?" Dad yelled. He was really mad.

"Hank and Zoey did it," said Dory.

"That does it," said Dad. "You can spend the rest of the morning doing chores."

First they had to wash piles of dishes.

**After** that they polished silverware.

Finally they had to sort old socks. Some of the socks had holes and smelled bad.

It was a miserable job.

To make things worse, when they finished,
Dory was still in the pool.
"That does it," said Hank. "We'll get our pool back
if it's the last thing we do."

They went to the front porch to think.

Just then some teenagers came by.

"Hey, where are you going?" asked Hank.

"To the town pool," said one.

Hank and Zoey looked at each other.

"Why go to a crowded town pool when you can have
one in your own backyard?" said Zoey.

"What do you mean?" asked another.
"Come on. We'll show you," said Hank.

They all went into the backyard.

"Yoo hoo, Dory. You have company," Zoey shouted.

"Ha, ha, look at Dory, queen of the baby pool."
Everyone started laughing.

"Eek!" said Dory.  She threw a towel
over her head and ran to the house.

Hank and Zoey got into the pool.

It was the coolest place in town.